ABSOLUTELY ANGELS

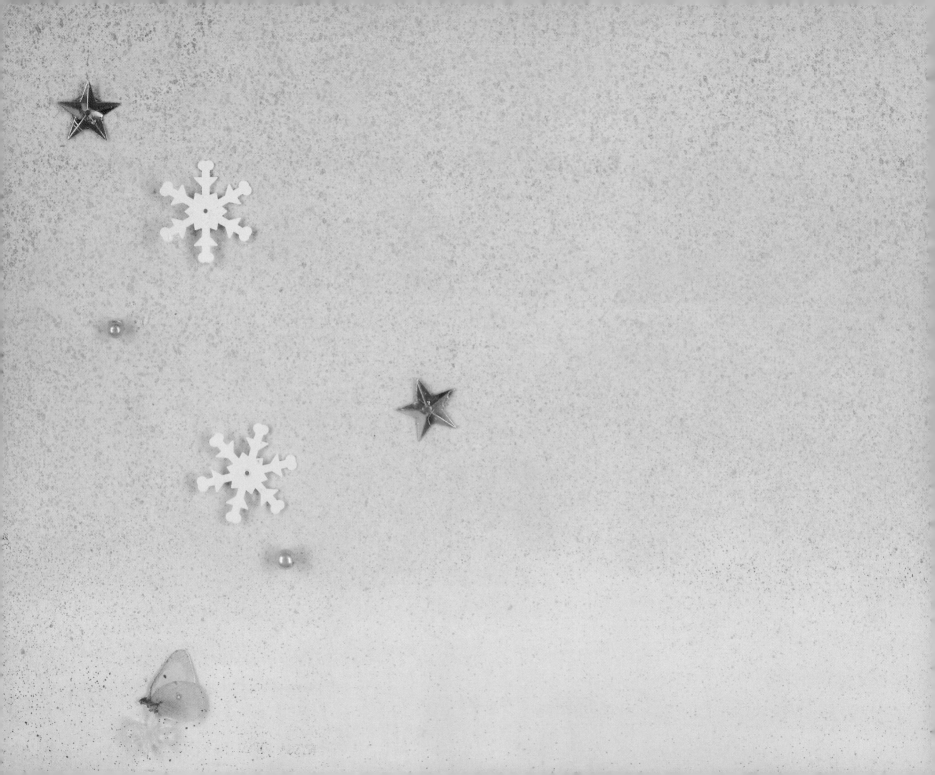

ABSOLUTELY ANGELS

POEMS FOR CHILDREN AND OTHER BELIEVERS

Selected by Mary Lou Carney

Illustrated by Viqui Maggio

WORDSONG

BOYDS MILLS PRESS

To my mother, who resides among angels
—M. L. C.

To big Sue, my angel
— V. M.

"Angels" copyright © 1992 by Valerie Worth.
Used by permission of HarperCollins
Publishers/Michael di Capna Books.

Published by Wordsong
Boyds Mills Press, Inc.
A Highlights Company
815 Church Street
Honesdale, Pennsylvania 18431
Printed in Mexico

First edition, 1998
Book designed by Tim Gillner
The text of this book is set in 13.5-point Cochin
The illustrations are mixed medium.

10 9 8 7 6 5 4 3 2 1

Text copyright © 1998 by Mary Lou Carney
Illustrations copyright © 1998 by Viqui Maggio
All rights reserved

Publisher Cataloging-in-Publication Data
Carney, Mary Lou
    Absolutely angels / by Mary Lou Carney ;
illustrated by Viqui Maggio.—1st ed.
[32]p. : col. ill. ; cm.
Summary: The glory and mystery of angels is the theme
of this collection of poems.
ISBN 1-56397-708-7
1. Children's poetry, American. 2. Angels—Juvenile poetry.
[1. American poetry. 2. Angels—Poetry] I. Maggio, Viqui, ill.
II. Title.
808.81 / 9382—dc 21   1998   AC   CIP
Library of Congress Catalog Card Number 97-77906

foreword

The earth is full of wonderful things. Miraculous things. Unseen things . . . like angels.

Could the summer breeze that ruffles your hair be the touch of an angel? Or the glow you notice as you drift off to sleep more than simply your night light? And what about the flimsy fence that somehow holds back that vicious dog?

Angels?

The Bible shows them as messengers and warriors. Artists have painted them as creatures full of beauty and grace. Hollywood movies have even given us baseball-playing ones.

What are angels *really* like? Powerful, of course. But perhaps they're a lot like you and me, too. Each one different and special, touched by God and given important work to do.

So come read about angels. Wide-winged, toe-tapping, safe-keeping angels. And if you turn the pages softly enough, you just may hear some heavenly humming.

—Mary Lou Carney

Divine Duties

High in the heavens
A loud rush of wings
As angels assemble
Before the Great King.

He stands tall before them
And holds out His hand.
"Go, do My bidding
Throughout all the land.

Protect all My people,
Defend right from wrong.
In tall pine trees whistle
My praise all day long.

The forces of evil
Defeat with My might—
And kiss every child
On the forehead tonight."

So quickly they scatter,
These creatures of light,
To do heaven's bidding
And bring earth delight.

—*Mary Lou Carney*

Night Angels

All over the cities,
all over the towns,
the angels are flying
in silvery gowns;
catching a whisper—
collecting a prayer,
their pockets are heavy
(but angels don't care)
and crossing the sky
they circle and soar,
to make their delivery
at heaven's front door.

—*Rebecca Kai Dotlich*

Angel Eyes

Angels are in Singapore,
and angels are in Maine.
Angels are in Istanbul,
and heaven makes it plain
that angel eyes are everywhere.
Around the world they see
through windows of the universe
to keep their watch on me.

—*Rebecca Kai Dotlich*

Tree-Top Angel

Tree-top angel
Silver bright,
You remind us
Of the light
At the time
Of Jesus' birth
And His blessing:
"Peace on Earth."
May that Christmas
Blessing stay
Even when you're
Tucked away.

—*Eileen Spinelli*

My Guardian Angel

Dear angel ever at my side,
how lovely you must be
To leave your home in heaven
to guard a child like me.

When I am far away from home,
or maybe hard at play—
I know you will protect me
from harm along the way.

Your beautiful and shining face
I see not, though you're near,
The sweetness of your lovely voice,
I cannot really hear.

When I pray you're praying too,
your prayer is just for me.
But when I sleep, you never do.
You're watching over me.

—*Author Unknown*

Baby's Angel

It's dark outside
Daddy ain't home
Mama's got the baby
Rockin', Rockin'
Mama's got the baby
Rockin'

The baby's sick
His fever's high
And doctor wants too
much
Money, Money
Doctor wants too much
Money

So Mama rocks
And Mama prays
Sings sweet songs about
Jesus, Jesus
Sings sweet songs about
Jesus

But Baby gets worse
He wails and moans
His fever starts to
Ragin', Ragin'
His fever starts to
Ragin'

Then all at once
He sits up straight
Laughs and goes to
Pointin', Pointin'
Laughs and goes to
Pointin'

Mama and me
Don't see a thing
But Baby lays back
Sighin', Sighin'
Baby lays back
Sighin'

Mama feels his brow—
It's cool as silk
And Baby has gone to
Sleepin', Sleepin'
Baby has gone to
Sleepin'

"Glory be!"
Mama whispers low
"Baby done seen an
Angel, Angel
Baby done seen an
Angel!"

—*Vicki L. Couch*

Angel in My House

There is an angel in my house,
an angel quiet as a mouse,
an angel in a golden gown,
who watches over me.

There is an angel in the hall,
an angel so completely small,
an angel with a halo crown,
who watches over me.

There is an angel in my room,
an angel gold as any moon,
an angel sitting solitaire,
who watches over me.

—Rebecca Kai Dotlich

Angels

Watching from
Heaven, they
Float on the
Spangled air:

The great
Sheaves of
Plumage at
Their shoulders

Serenely folded,
One long
Gleaming feather
Over another.

—*Valerie Worth*

Unseen Angels

I've never really seen one,
with wings and such, I mean.
I think they might
be silver-white,
not apricot
or green.

In pictures they
have halos,
that gleam
and glitter gold;
they carry tiny trumpets —
sometimes they carry scrolls.

I've never really seen one,
but there's one guarantee —
heaven says they've sent them,
and that's enough
for me.

—*Rebecca Kai Dotlich*

The Real Thing

Angel stickers,
Angel stamps.
Angel nightlights,
Angel lamps.

Angel cookies,
Angel cards.
Angel statues
In our yards.

But *real* angels?
Do you suppose
We'd recognize
One of those?

—*Lisa Bahlinger*

Recital

Angels dancing in the dark
beneath my bedroom window,
bare feet tapping to the tune
that's humming in my mind.
Moonlight spotlights silver wings,
unfolded in a pirouette.

How can I sleep
when so close by
angels dance
the minuet?

—*Mary Lou Carney*

Evening Prayer

Now I lay me down to sleep,
I pray, dear Lord, my soul you'll keep.
May angels watch me through the night
And wake me with the morning light.

Amen.

GLORIA IN EXCELSIS DEO

Christmas

A star celebration
come down to earth.
Celestial fireworks
announcing his birth.

Hosts of bright angels
With blinding white light
Proclaim to the world:
Tonight is the night!

—*Mary Lou Carney*

Getting Dressed

Maybe angels put on bodies
the way we put on clothes—
        with buttons and
            zippers and
                bows

But underneath,
    pulsing power
    and
        dazzling glow.

—Lisa Bahlinger

A Clean Sweep

When Isabel lay down to sleep,
she prayed the Lord her soul to keep
safe from the monster under her bed.
(He's purple slime with a big green head!)
Her monster's tricky and turns to air.
When Mother looks, he's never there.

Isabel's angel already knew
exactly what she had to do.
She floated down to Isabel's room
and brought a sharp and prickly broom.
She poked and prodded under the bed.
The monster yelped and yowled—and fled.

Isabel's monster ran out of town.
Isabel's angel brushed off her gown.
She smiled and whispered, "All is well.
Now go to sleep, my sweet Isabel."

—*Diana Smith*

Request

Angel sitting on a star
we have left our door ajar.
Come and share the cozy light
of our kitchen hearth tonight.
Bring your goodness,
grace and song.
Bring your dancing wings along.
By the fire's peaceful glow
teach us what we need to know.

—*Eileen Spinelli*

Michael's Angel

I saw an angel's picture
in an antique frame of gold.
He was a warrior angel
with a face both fierce and bold.

My guardian angel looks like that—
he waves a flaming sword of light
and clears my room of gruesome things
that lurk beneath my bed at night.

What did he do before I came?
Protect a prophet, guard a king?
Bring messages from God to earth?
Show shepherds how to use a sling?

And does he really talk to God,
up personal and face-to-face?
Has he traveled to a star
that winks at me from outer space?

I wonder if he picked me out
from all the boys he might have chose.
Does he like the things I like?
Can he teach me what he knows?

My angel is a soldier brave
who fights in highest heaven's host
defending goodness, right and light—
but I bet he guards me the most!

—Sailor Metts

Morning Prayer

Angel of God
    my guardian dear,

To whom God's love
    commits me here,

Ever this day
    be at my side,

To light and guard,
    to rule and guide.

Amen.

Whisper of Angel Wings

Today I stumbled and once again
Was lifted up by an unseen hand.
What comfort and joy that knowledge brings.
For I hear the whisper of angel wings.

The guardian angels God sends to all
To bear us up when we stumble and fall.
Trust Him, my friend, and often you'll hear
The whisper of angel wings hovering near.

—*Author Unknown*

Angel Bouquets

Angels, in the early morning
May be seen the Dews among,
Stooping—plucking—smiling—flying—
Do the Buds to them belong?

Angels, when the sun is hottest
May be seen the sands among,
Stooping—plucking—sighing—flying—
Parched the flowers they bear along.

—*Emily Dickinson*

Little League Angel

I squint through sunlight at the ball
Hit at least a full mile high.
The wind has caught it! Now it's tumbling
Quickly, wildly from the sky.

I'll never catch it! Here it comes,
Dropping like a heavy stone.
I duck my head, then—suddenly—
begin to feel I'm not alone.

I shove my glove above my head
As nearer comes the hurtling ball
Dipping, darting, spinning fast—
I see it fall, but that's not all…

A pure white cloud moves overhead
and comes between the sun and me.
Then changes to a vision that
the sunspots won't quite let me see.

I watch the ball fall to my glove,
I feel a pressure make it stay.
And I could swear that cloud at once
Turned and bowed and flew away.

I've heard that guardian angels
Watch over children every day.
But I know mine did more than watch—
He helped me start a double play!

—*Gene Fehler*

Weather Report

Do you suppose
    when a raindrop hits your nose
    you've been kissed by an angel?

Do you suppose
    when it snows
    angels are having pillow fights?

Do you suppose
    anyone knows
    for sure?

—*Mary Lou Carney*

Snow Angels

Do snow angels shiver
when it's thirty-one below,
or does the windchill matter
when your wings are made of snow?

And do they rise to guard our yard
while frozen night winds blow
their icy halos round and round
at thirty-one below?

—*Mary Lou Carney*

Where Angels Watch

Tonight in the sky
there's a billion bright stars.
When angels are watching,
is that where they are?
Is that where they go
to watch over me—
are stars
front row chairs
for the angels to see?

—Rebecca Kai Dotlich

No Peeping

I cannot tell
If I'm awake
Or if in sleep I hear
The rustling
Of angel wings
Whispering in my ear.
I try to keep
My eyes shut tight;
They mustn't see me peep—
For when I wake
They fly away
Till next time
I'm asleep.

—Vicki L. Couch

Goodnight Angel

Goodnight angel,
if I weep,
do dry my tears
that I might
sleep.

—*Rebecca Kai Dotlich*